The Crazy Cousins
first published in 2012
this edition published in 2017 by
Hardie Grant Egmont
Ground Floor, Building 1, 658 Church Street
Richmond, Victoria 3121, Australia
www.hardiegrantegmont.com.au

A CiP record for this title is available from the National Library of Australia

Text copyright © 2012 Sally Rippin
Illustration copyright © 2012 Stephanie Spartels
Logo and design copyright © 2012 Hardie Grant Egmont

Design by Stephanie Spartels
Typesetting by Michaela Stone

Printed in China through Asia Pacific Offset

1 3 5 4 2

The Crazy Cousins

By Sally Rippin

Illustrated by Stephanie Spartels

hardie grant EGMONT

Chapter One

This is Jack. Today Jack
is in a moochy mood.
When he is in a moochy
mood, Jack likes to play
all by himself.

Jack is playing with his
Lego. He has built an
enormous castle with
a moat. Now he must
save all the people in
the castle from the
fierce dragon.

Jack's dad knocks on
the door. 'Hey, Jack,'
he says.

'Don't forget that your cousins are coming over today. You had better get dressed!'

Jack sits up. His cousins? Oh no! He *had* forgotten!

Jack has the noisiest, **messiest** cousins in the whole world.

He is *definitely* not in
the mood for his cousins
today.

Jack **frowns**.

'Do they have to come?'
he asks his dad. 'Last time
David broke my remote-
control car. Stella drew
on my maths book.
And Ivy picked all
Mum's flowers!'

Jack's dad smiles. 'They're
your cousins, Jack.'

7

'And we don't see them often,' his dad adds.

'You'll have to try to get along. Why don't you invite Billie over, too?'

Billie is Jack's best friend. She lives next door.

'Good idea,' says Jack. He pulls on some clothes and runs downstairs.

But then he remembers.
Billie said she was going
to play at Rebecca's
house today.

Oh no! Three annoying
cousins and no best friend.
What a **disaster**.

Jack's tummy begins to
jump about like a frog.
Soon it starts to hurt.

Jack creeps upstairs
and crawls into bed.
He pulls the blanket
up over his head.
All he wanted was
a quiet, moochy day.
Now the noisiest,
craziest cousins
ever are on their
way over.

11

Jack lies in bed
and imagines all
the **terrible**
things they will get
up to this time.

Chapter Two

Soon, Jack's dad
knocks on the door.
'Jack?' he calls softly.
'Come on. Your cousins
have arrived!'

'Tell them I'm not here,'
Jack says from under
the blanket.

Jack's dad comes into the
room. He sits down on
the end of the bed.

15

'They're here to see you, Jack,' he says.

Jack sighs. Then he kicks off the blanket and follows his dad downstairs.

In the kitchen, Jack's uncle and aunt are talking with his mum. Suddenly they hear a **scream**.

Everyone looks outside.
David is chasing Stella
and Ivy with a stick.

'David!' calls Jack's
Uncle Bob.

'That's enough!'
Aunty Bee calls.

But Jack's cousins
don't listen. They run
around the garden
like little monsters.

Jack sighs. Why does
he have to play with
his annoying cousins?
They are the worst
cousins in the world!

He walks outside
and sits down on
the back step.
He wishes Billie was
here to help him.

A best friend always
makes things better.

'Hey Jack!' David calls.
'Do you want to
play soccer?'

'No,' says Jack grumpily.
'Last time you kicked my
soccer ball over the fence!'

'How about we make a
potion then?' says Ivy.
'Remember we made
one last time?'

'We got in **trouble** because you picked all Mum's flowers,' Jack says, frowning. 'I don't want to make a potion again.'

'I'm sorry,' says Ivy in a little voice. She flops down on the back step beside Jack.

David kicks a pebble
and Stella chews her
fingernails. The three of
them look miserable.

'We just want to play
with you,' Stella says
to Jack.

'You're the one with all
the good ideas,' David says.

'Yeah, Jack!' Ivy says.
'You're the bestest,
funnest cousin
in the whole wide world.'

Jack looks up at his
cousins in surprise.

The best cousin?
He didn't know
they thought that!

Jack gets a warm honey feeling in his tummy. Now he feels bad for acting so **grumpy**.

He certainly hasn't been the best cousin today. He's been the *worst* cousin!

'Well,' he says slowly, 'I guess you could come and look at my Lego castle.'

'Really?' says David.

Jack grins. 'It's got a tower and a moat and even a drawbridge!'

'Cool!' shout Stella
and Ivy together.

Jack smiles and the four
of them run upstairs
to his bedroom.

Chapter Three

When Jack's cousins see his castle, they all gasp.

'Wow!' says David.

'That's so cool!' says Stella.

Jack feels very proud.

'Can we play with it?'
Ivy says, jumping
up and down in
excitement.

'Ummm…' says Jack. His tummy starts to wriggle around again.

He doesn't want his cousins to touch his Lego castle in case they break it. But he doesn't want to be mean either. Jack doesn't know what to do.

'Um, all right,' says Jack.
'But be careful.'

'Can I be the knight?'
David says.

'Can I be the princess?'
Stella says.

'Can I be the dragon?'
Ivy shouts.

She picks up the dragon
and **SWOOPS** it
towards the castle tower.

'Oh no!' says Jack.

But it's too late.

Ivy crashes the dragon
into the tower and
all the little pieces of
Lego tumble down
to the ground.

David and Stella freeze.
Their eyes grow wide
in fright.

Little Ivy covers her face in her hands and begins to cry.

'I'm sorry!' she says.

'I didn't mean to break your castle, Jack.'

Jack looks at Ivy. He looks at David and Stella too. He remembers what they said to him outside and the big moochy, grumpy bubble inside him **pops**. He smiles.

'That's OK, Ivy,' he says.

'It was an accident.

Anyway, Lego is *meant*

to be broken. Look!'

Jack picks up another
dragon and crashes
it into the wall of
the castle. The wall
breaks into tiny pieces.
Jack's cousins look
nervous.

Jack giggles. Then he
crashes his
dragon into the
other wall.

Another part of
the castle comes
tumbling down.

'Come on!' says Jack, laughing. 'You can break the rest, Ivy.'

Ivy crashes her dragon into the last wall.

The castle is now in **ruins**. Little Lego pieces lie everywhere.

'What now?' says David. He still looks worried.

'Well, now we build
it again, of course!'
Jack laughs.

So Jack and his
cousins build another
castle, taller than
the last one. This time
it is Stella's turn to
crash it down.
Stella and Ivy and
David laugh loudly.

Jack laughs the **loudest** of all.

All afternoon Jack and his cousins build castles out of Lego, then crash them down again. It's the best afternoon ever!

Hey Jack! The Crazy Cousins By Sally Rippin

Hey Jack! The Scary Solo By Sally Rippin

Hey Jack! The Winning Goal By Sally Rippin

Hey Jack! The Robot Blues By Sally Rippin

Hey Jack! The Worry Monsters By Sally Rippin

Hey Jack! The New Friend By Sally Rippin

Hey Jack! The Worst Sleepover By Sally Rippin

Hey Jack! The Lost Reindeer By Sally Rippin

Hey Jack! The Circus Lesson By Sally Rippin

Hey Jack! The Bumpy Ride By Sally Rippin

Hey Jack! The Top Team By Sally Rippin

Hey Jack! The Playground Problem By Sally Rippin

Hey Jack! The Best Party Ever By Sally Rippin

Hey Jack! The Big Adventure By Sally Rippin

Hey Jack! The Bravest Kid By Sally Rippin

Hey Jack! The Toy Sale By Sally Rippin

Hey Jack! The Other Teacher By Sally Rippin

Hey Jack! The Party Invite By Sally Rippin

Hey Jack! The Extra-special Group By Sally Rippin

Hey Jack! The Star of the Week By Sally Rippin